BOOK #2

WEDNESDAY & WOOF

NEW PUP ON
THE BLOCK

Check out more Wednesday and Woof mysteries!

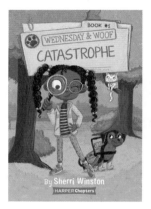 

BOOK #2

WEDNESDAY & WOOF

NEW PUP ON
THE BLOCK

By SHERRI WINSTON

Illustrated by
GLADYS JOSE

HARPER
An Imprint of HarperCollinsPublishers

TO MY GREAT NEPHEW,
STEVEN ANTHONY WINSTON JR.
THE NEXT GENERATION OF LITERACY AND LOVE.

Library of Congress Control Number: 2021948133
ISBN 978-0-06-297607-9 — ISBN 978-0-06-297606-2 (pbk.)

Typography by Alice Wang and Catherine Lee
21 22 23 24 25   RTLO   10 9 8 7 6 5 4 3 2 1

First Edition

TABLE of CONTENTS

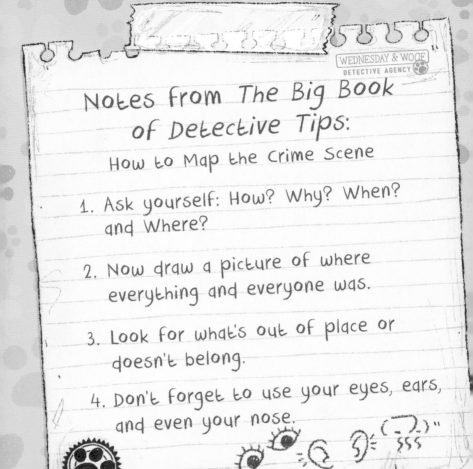

Notes from *The Big Book of Detective Tips:*

How to Map the Crime Scene

1. Ask yourself: How? Why? When? and Where?

2. Now draw a picture of where everything and everyone was.

3. Look for what's out of place or doesn't belong.

4. Don't forget to use your eyes, ears, and even your nose.

WEDNESDAY & WOOF
DETECTIVE AGENCY

CHAPTER #1

STICKY
FINGERS!

"**MAY WE** interview the twins?" I ask.

Mrs. PomPom frowns as we climb her front porch. Five minutes ago, she ran into my yard yelling that she'd been robbed and needed help. Believe it or not, that happens to me a lot.

I am Wednesday Walia Nadir, the number one detective in our neighborhood. My dog, Woof, is my partner in the Wednesday and Woof Detective Agency.

"Interview? But they are just kindergartners, Wednesday," she says. "What could they possibly know about thieving crooks who break into old ladies' homes and steal their precious orange candy-making syrup?"

"I think the twins can help," I answer as we enter her cozy home. A good detective needs the facts. The twins are Mrs. Pom-Pom's grandchildren: Zuri and Zach. They were the only other people in the house when the syrup went missing.

Woof gently rubs his nose against my hand, his signal that I need my detective's notebook. I reach inside his vest pocket and grab it.

But my new friend Mariposa speaks first.

"Show us the scene of the crime!" she demands. "I love reading detective stories like the Shirley Hurley books. She's the best at solving mysteries! Me and Ruthie are learning to be detectives, too!"

Mariposa's new support dog, Ruthie, *sniff-sniff-sniffs* Mrs. PomPom's hands and a few empty syrup jars. Woof nudges Ruthie, and

she soon calms down. Woof is a very good role model.

"I like your silver shoes," Zuri tells Mariposa as she leads us to the room she shares with her brother. Mariposa really does have amazing sparkly shoes. She's pretty stylish.

"Why does your dog keep sniffing?" Zach asks Mariposa.

"It's her job," says Mariposa.

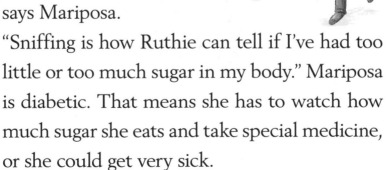

"Sniffing is how Ruthie can tell if I've had too little or too much sugar in my body." Mariposa is diabetic. That means she has to watch how much sugar she eats and take special medicine, or she could get very sick.

Zuri grins. "If Grandma had that kind of dog, its nose would fall off from sniffing Zach because of all the sugar he eats!" We all laugh as we sit around the small table. Zach sits crisscross on the floor.

"Hey, Zuri, love your room," I say. "Were you having a tea party?"

She nods. "This morning. Zach didn't play 'cause he had a sick tummy," she says. Zach looks away. I follow his gaze to his bed.

It sits high off the floor and has big drawers underneath.

"Zach," I begin softly, "are you feeling okay now?" He looks sort of miserable.

Zach shrugs.

"Nothing wrong with me or my tummy," he mumbles. "I didn't want to play tea party. I wanted to play pirate."

Hmm, I wonder . . .

Ruthie jumps off the floor, sniffing and licking him more.

"Down, girl," says Mariposa. "She's not supposed to do that. She's still learning." Ruthie continues to *sniff-sniff-sniff* at Zach.

I make a list of clues in my notebook. I detect a faint orange scent in the room. I look at Woof. He nods. Yep, he smells it, too. It could mean the thief was here!

"Zuri, can you show us your favorite treasure?" Mariposa asks. I smile at Mariposa. I wonder if she's seeing the same clues I'm seeing.

Zuri grabs a small shoebox from the closet.

She opens the shoebox to show her treasures—marbles, a few rocks, two doll shoes, and crayons.

"That's good stuff," I say, then I turn to Zach. "I'll bet her hiding place is way better than yours."

"Is not!" he says, shooting to his feet.

"Bet it is!" Mariposa says. "Let us see!"

Soon as he moves, Ruthie sticks her nose in his fingers. "I think she likes me," Zach says.

Woof moves toward the drawers under Zach's bed. He takes another long sniff.

When Zach opens one of the drawers, I

hear a tinkling sound. Glass bottles, I'd bet.

"Arf! Arf! Arf!" says Ruthie.

"Woof!" says Woof.

"The dogs can smell the orange oil scent," I say. "Zach, it's on your skin."

"Aha!" Mariposa shouts. "Caught you red-handed!" She's still learning the detective biz, but she's right.

"Zach," I say, "is there something you'd like to tell your grandmother?"

ONE CHAPTER DOWN, AND ONE MYSTERY IS ALREADY SOLVED. OFF TO A GREAT START!

CHAPTER #2

WINS BY
A "HARE"!

"THAT WAS awesome!" Mariposa says as we walk to my house. Mariposa's family just moved in a few houses away. "When did you know?"

"Well, like it says in *The Big Book of Detective Tips*, I had to use my eyes, ears, and even my nose," I say. "Only three people were home. I saw how Zach was acting mopey, almost guilty. Zuri said Zach had a big sweet tooth.

And both Woof and Ruthie could smell something on Zach's side of the room—*and* on his fingers."

"Oooh, you're good, Wednesday Nadir!" Mariposa says. We give each other high fives. Our smiles are wide. "But I bet you aren't better than the detective in my favorite book, *Shirley Hurley and the Case of the Missing Classroom*," she says.

"I am better, because I'm real!" I say with a grin.

14

"Woof!" says my number one assistant and support dog, Woof.

Ruthie jumps and barks, "Arf! Arf! Arf!"

"Hey, Wednesday!" comes a shout. Me and Mariposa turn to see someone hopping toward us.

"That's my best friend, Belinda Bundy!" I say. Her pogo stick goes *boing-boing-boing*! "Sometimes we just call her Bunny. She hops a lot."

Belinda Bundy waves at Mariposa and me. She really wants to be a bunny when she grows up. Not a detective. Her parents do something called "creative parenting." Mom says we don't have that in our house.

"We're going to my house. Want to come?" I ask after introducing her to Mariposa.

"Sure!" says Belinda. She turns and points her pogo stick toward my house. "Race ya!"

I run my fastest, feeling the air in my lungs and sun on my face. Woof races beside me, his support vest flapping, ready to help if I need it. Belinda Bundy wins.

Mariposa says, "No fair! She used a pogo stick!"

"Belinda hops everywhere. That stick is like her shoes." I laugh. Mariposa and Belinda laugh, too.

When we reach my front yard, Raafe, my twin brother, and his friend Calvin run to meet us.

"Your grandpa is going to let us play with the drones in the backyard," Calvin says. Daddy bought Raafe a drone with a remote control, and Grandpa bought some smaller ones so we could play with our friends.

"Cool!" me and Belinda Bundy say at the same time.

"Awesome!" says Mariposa. Ruthie is *sniff-sniff-sniffing* her again.

I rub the top of Woof's head, and he knows what to do. He goes over and walks around Ruthie in a circle. He nudges her until he has her attention.

"Do you need to eat?" I ask Mariposa. Food is sort of like medicine for her.

If her meter beeps, it means she could pass out if she doesn't get some quick sugar.

"I think, yeah, maybe I do," she says. She pulls a thermos of fruit juice from her backpack and takes a sip. Then she tucks her backpack under the table. "*Ahhh!* Okay, I'm ready."

I give Woof the hand signal for *sit*. "Sit!"

Woof obeys, and soon Ruthie is sitting, too. Then I give the signal for *stay*. Woof nods. Ruthie whines.

"Sorry," says Mariposa. "I haven't had her long, and I can't remember all the hand signals."

"You'll get it," I say.

Then comes a voice that makes me grit my teeth. "Oh no! Not another poopy puppy on the block."

Woof growls.

I turn around.

"Anita B. Moo-see-apricot!" I say.

CHAPTER #3

MISSING IMPOSSIBLE!

"IT'S PRONOUNCED Moose-E-A, Wednesday Nadir. You know that," Anita growls. Gruff, her bossy dog, growls, too. Woof moves to stand in front of me. *Good boy.*

Anita B. picks up Raafe's drone. "It's not so cool," she says. Raafe gently takes it away from her. I roll my eyes.

Calvin sighs and says, "Um, Anita, want to play, too?"

"Well . . . ," she says, like she's got *soooooo* much to think about. "I guess I can stay a few minutes. Then I've got important things to do!" She chooses the last drone.

We play for the next hour chasing the floating, flying objects. Grandpa waves at us. The dogs bark and play. Everyone is having fun, even Anita B. Woof remains alert for signs of me getting too sore or tired because he's still on duty.

I have juvenile arthritis, and I have to be careful. Luckily, I have Woof to remind me to take breaks!

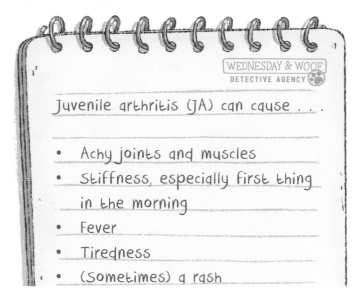

WEDNESDAY & WOOF
DETECTIVE AGENCY

Juvenile arthritis (JA) can cause . . .

- Achy joints and muscles
- Stiffness, especially first thing in the morning
- Fever
- Tiredness
- (Sometimes) a rash

Ruthie sniffs at Raafe's hand and then barks at the drone. Raafe laughs. "Maybe it smells like my lunch!"

"Eeew!" I say to Raafe. "That smell is gross. What is that?"

"Leftover lamb sandwich." He grins. "It's been in my backpack with the drone for a few days." Sometimes it's hard to believe he's *my* twin.

Woof gives Raafe's hand a sniff, too. "Woof!"

We're all laughing, even mean ol' Anita B., until we hear an awful screeching sound and turn toward the road.

"Look!" says Mariposa.

"Oh no! It looks like that truck is going to crash!" I say.

Turns out the old truck doesn't crash. It only loses a few apples after swerving. We place the drones on the grass near the patio. Grandpa comes out and walks over with us to make sure the driver is all right.

"See anything important over there?" Belinda calls from the opposite side of the truck.

When I bend down to pick up another apple, Woof leans into my leg to give me support. Belinda is looking under the truck, then her face disappears. I watch her shoes, gray sneakers with white bunnies, climb back onto the pogo stick and

hop back to the yard. I see everyone else's feet under the old truck, too.

Blue sneakers—that's Raafe; black lace-ups—Calvin; white with ponies—Anita B. I giggle. It's funny seeing only the bottoms of everybody. Woof smiles, too.

"I think everything's good here," Grandpa tells us. The driver nods and climbs back into his truck.

We wave and my stomach growls. Loudly. "Grandpa, it's time for our snacks!" I say.

"Race you back to the drones!" Raafe says. I'm trying to tell him I'm hungry when he breaks into a fast run. We all run after him.

"No fair! No fair!" I call out.

Of course, Raafe is first to reach the drones. I'm going to give him a piece of my mind—until I see his face.

He cries out, "My drone is missing!"

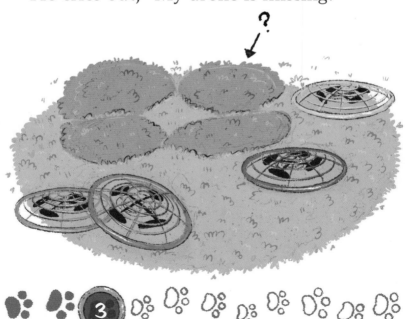

CHAPTER #4

A NEW MYSTERY
BEGINS

"OH NO!" I say, turning to Woof. "Don't worry, Raafe. The Wednesday and Woof Detective Agency is on the case!" Raafe looks sadder than that time a bug flew up his nose. We never saw that bug again.

Time for my notebook. Woof trots over, and I take it out of his vest again. "Good boy," I say. His tail *thump-thump-thumps* on the grass.

I look around to see who is here and try to get a mental picture of the scene of the crime.

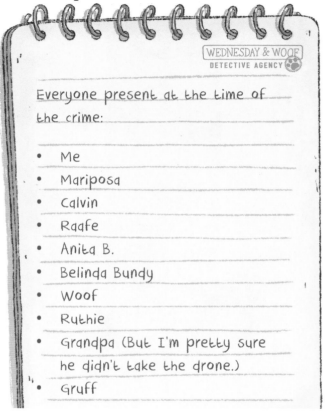

WEDNESDAY & WOOF
DETECTIVE AGENCY

Everyone present at the time of the crime:

- Me
- Mariposa
- Calvin
- Raafe
- Anita B.
- Belinda Bundy
- Woof
- Ruthie
- Grandpa (But I'm pretty sure he didn't take the drone.)
- Gruff

Woof nuzzles my arm. Not to play, but to remind me to sit the right way so I don't strain my back. "Good boy," I whisper.

Then I look around.

"Where is Ruthie?" I ask Mariposa.

"Ruthie!" she calls. No Ruthie.

Grandpa joins us. He looks concerned.

"Maybe someone, um, borrowed the drone while we were checking on the truck driver," he says. Not hardly. But a lightbulb in my brain goes FLASH!

Of course!

That was the only time we were all away from the drones.

"Grandpa, I think I can figure this out. I'm going to need everyone's cooperation," I say. "But first, I need to make a diagram."

"Ahh, very good idea, little one," he says with a smile. "Why don't you go to your boat office and ask yourself some important questions?"

Who? What? When? Where? How?

"That's exactly what my number one detective's book says I should do!" I say. Grandpa is very wise. "Mariposa, you can come with me. That is, if you still want to be a detective in training."

"Yes! Of course I am still a detective in training!" she says.

"Arf! Arf! Arf!" says Ruthie as she runs out from behind a tree.

YOU'VE ALREADY READ 2,168 WORDS. YOU MUST BE AS DETERMINED TO SOLVE THIS MYSTERY AS WEDNESDAY AND WOOF ARE!

CHAPTER #5

WHERE COULD RAAFE'S DRONE BE?

WE'RE STARTING toward my boat office when my legs feel weak. Woof is at my side quick as a flash. I steady myself with the small handle on the top of his vest.

"You okay?" asks Mariposa.

"I'm fine. Maybe I overdid it a teeny-tiny bit," I say.

"Serves you right," says Anita B., sneaking up behind me. I hate when she sneaks. "You know you shouldn't be running and racing.

Not with your *jubilee* arthritis."

"Gruff! Gruff!" says her grumpy dog, Gruff.

Sigh!

"It's called *ju-ve-nile* arthritis, or JA," I say. "And I can do anything that anyone else can. Sometimes I need to rest, that's all!"

"What do we do next?" Mariposa asks, pushing between me and Anita B. "I don't want to miss a minute of the mystery solving."

"First," I say, "we need to make a diagram of the crime scene."

"How?" Mariposa asks.

We leave Anita B. behind and climb into my office.

"Come here, Woof," I say, and my trusty assistant is right at my side. I get my crayons and notepad from his vest.

"See, Mariposa?" I say. "I have to try to remember where everyone was and draw a picture to show it." I start this one by drawing the patio, creating a sort of rect-angle.

"What are the circles for?" she asks, lean-ing over my shoulder to see.

"That's us. I need to know where everyone was standing when we heard the screech," I say.

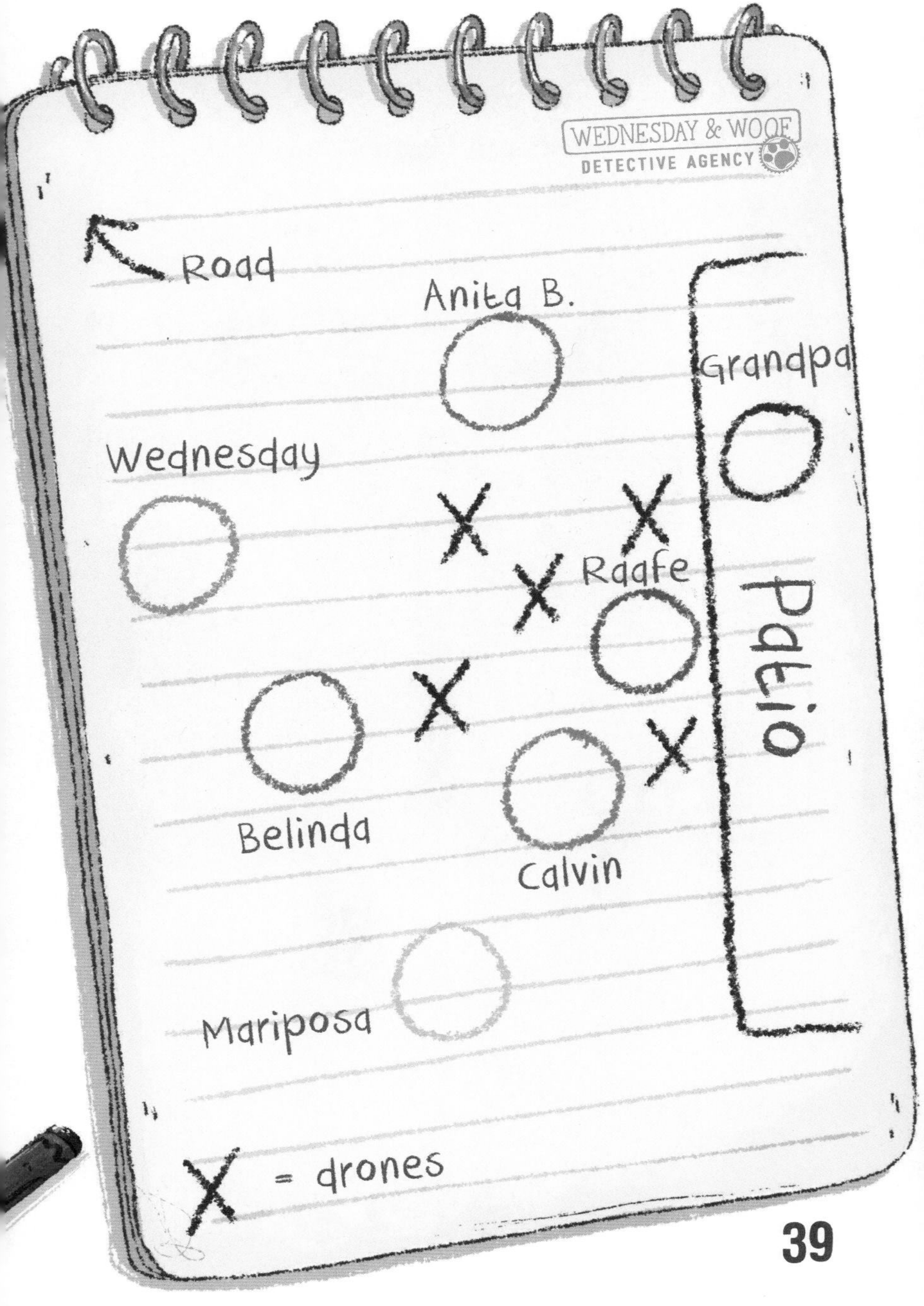

WEDNESDAY & WOOF
DETECTIVE AGENCY

Road

Anita B.

Grandpa

Wednesday

X   X

X   Raafe

Patio

X

X

Belinda

Calvin

Mariposa

X = drones

39

"Shirley Hurley made a map in *The Case of the Stolen Gems*," says Mariposa. "I love making maps."

"Me too," I tell her, looking at the paper in front of me. "But right now, we have to think. Where could Raafe's drone be?"

CHAPTER #6
LOOKING FOR EVIDENCE

"WOOF, WE need to ask questions," I say. "We need to figure out how, why, when, where, and who—just like we did at Mrs. PomPom's house. Let's get everybody to the patio."

Woof nods. It's a trick I taught him when he was still a puppy. It's easy to learn.

I check my notebook:

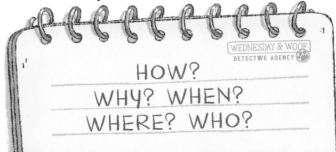

HOW?
WHY? WHEN?
WHERE? WHO?

WEDNESDAY & WOOF
DETECTIVE AGENCY

41

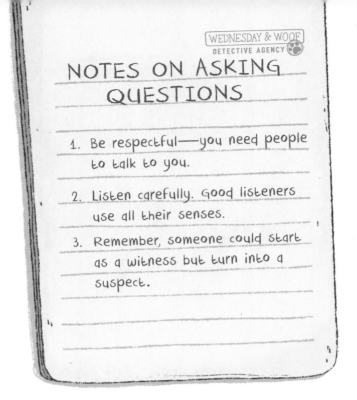

WEDNESDAY & WOOF
DETECTIVE AGENCY

NOTES ON ASKING QUESTIONS

1. Be respectful—you need people to talk to you.

2. Listen carefully. Good listeners use all their senses.

3. Remember, someone could start as a witness but turn into a suspect.

With the notepad tucked under my arm, Mariposa and I go back to the patio. Woof and Ruthie follow close-by. "Grandpa, it's time for questions—and answers!" I say.

"An excellent idea!" he agrees. He calls to the others, "Children, come to the patio, please."

42

Raafe, Calvin, Belinda Bundy, and even Anita B. dash across the lawn to join me and Mariposa. Once everybody gathers around the patio table, I show them my diagram.

"I've marked where all of us were playing before the screeching tires. Now I need to figure out what happened next," I say.

Woof moves closer in case I need any other supplies from the pockets of his vest.

"This is so cool!" Mariposa squeals and claps her hands. Ruthie barks and jumps up to try to lick her fingers.

"I'm a better drawer," grumbles Anita B., looking at the circles and Xs on the diagram. It's best not to listen too closely to Anita B. "And hurry up. I have something important to do!"

Belinda looks at me and shrugs, our signal that Anita B. is being really, really Moose-ish!

Woof gives me my pencil and I get back to work. "Raafe," I say, "tell me the last time you saw your drone."

"Well, I was standing right there," he says, pointing to the circle nearest to the patio. "I heard the screeching, set the drone down, and took off running."

I look at the map. "And you're sure you laid it down right there? Near the edge of the patio?"

He nodded. "I'm sure!" he says.

"Were you the first one to reach the truck?" I ask.

Raafe bites his lip. He makes a thinking

face. "Well . . . ," he says, "yes! Me and Calvin were tied."

"We were the fastest!" says Calvin. The boys high-five.

"Oh, I know!" says Mariposa. "If we figure out who was last, we'll find the thief!"

CHAPTER 7

YOU MUST BE THE CROOK!

I ASK each person what they remember about the moments before the drone went missing.

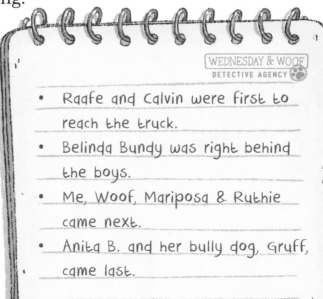

WEDNESDAY & WOOF
DETECTIVE AGENCY

- Raafe and Calvin were first to reach the truck.
- Belinda Bundy was right behind the boys.
- Me, Woof, Mariposa & Ruthie came next.
- Anita B. and her bully dog, Gruff, came last.

"Did anyone see anything suspicious?" I ask. They all shake their heads. My eyes scan the distance from the patio to the road.

I glance at the circles. Calvin understands what I'm doing.

"The blue circle was closest to the road and could have gotten there fast and gotten back fast, too," he says.

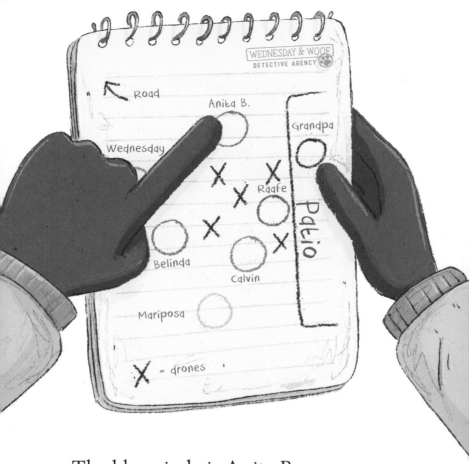

The blue circle is Anita B.

Hmm . . .

"So doesn't this mean the blue circle is probably the person who took the drone?" Mariposa asks.

"Well . . . ," I say, "it might mean that or—"

But Mariposa jumps ahead. "That's how it goes in mystery books—especially in *Shirley Hurley and the Case of the Stolen Bird.* Know what it means?" she asks. She points at Anita B. and says, "It means *you* must be the crook!"

"Am not!" squawks Anita B.

"Are you *suuuuuuuure?*" Mariposa says, making *sure* sound like an extra-extra-long word.

As much as Anita B. bugs me, I don't think it's right to accuse her. At least, not without proof.

"Mariposa, we're not accusing anybody," I tell her. "We're just asking questions."

"She could have taken the drone when we weren't looking," she says.

"That's true," I say. "But we don't have enough facts yet."

I want to say more, only I notice Mariposa's skin looking pale and her cheeks sort of flushed.

"Arf! Arf! Arf!" says Ruthie. She tugs at the bottom of Mariposa's jacket.

"I think Ruthie is trying to tell you something," I say. "Hey, remember when Ruthie disappeared for a little while earlier? Where was she?"

"She didn't do this!" Mariposa says.

"Well, maybe she just hid it. Like a game."

Ruthie barks, "Arf! Arf! Arf!" And again she tugs on Mariposa's jacket.

"You look funny," Anita B. says to Mariposa. She's right.

"Are you okay?" I ask Mariposa.

"I need my . . . ," Mariposa says. She tries to walk, but she wobbles . . .

54

CRASH! Mariposa falls down on her bottom!

YOU'RE MORE THAN HALFWAY THROUGH! HOW MANY CLUES HAVE YOU COUNTED SO FAR?

7

CHAPTER #8

TRUTH OR CONSEQUENCES

"OH NO!" says Belinda Bundy.

We rush to Mariposa's side. "Are you okay?" I ask. "Do you want some water?" I can feel my heart beating really fast. I hope she's not sick.

"Arf! Arf! Arf!" barks Ruthie.

"Your dog is going goofy!" Anita B. says, her worried eyes looking from Mariposa to Ruthie and back again. The puppy keeps barking—stopping—then barking again.

Is she giving a signal?

"We're okay, aren't we, girl?" Mariposa says, fluffing Ruthie's fur. "I just need to get another snack out of my bag."

"I can get it for you," says Raafe.

"NO!" Mariposa shouts. Then she looks guilty for yelling and says, "Sorry. I can get it on my own, thank you."

"Gee, you sure are touchy," Anita B. says, but she reaches out to help Mariposa up. Anita B. can be normal sometimes.

"Ruthie might be trying to alert you that something is wrong. Shouldn't you check your blood-sugar meter?" I ask.

Ruthie nods. So does Woof. Honest, they both really do.

Mariposa stands slowly, and Woof follows her outside the patio door where she left her bag, making sure she doesn't fall—just like he does for me. She brings it back to the table, pulls out a string cheese, then stuffs the bag under the table.

Ruthie whimpers, then sits at attention. Woof nods his approval. Ruthie is going to be a good support dog. Just like Woof.

"No wonder Ruthie was barking so much," says Mariposa, pulling up her shirt to check the little rectangle of plastic clipped to her belt loop. "I must've set my meter too high. I'm getting too much insulin." She touches her monitor and it beeps.

"Ruthie is trained to tell when I'm getting too much or not enough!"

"You did a great job, Ruthie!" I say.

"Arf! Arf!" Ruthie barks as Grandpa comes onto the patio carrying a tray with glasses of lemonade. He also has bottled waters.

"Are you okay, little butterfly?" he asks, pointing to the butterfly on Mariposa's shirt.

Mariposa giggles. "My name means butterfly in Spanish," she says. "I'm feeling better. I need to eat a little snack."

"Well, children, why don't the rest of you break for a beverage," Grandpa says with a wide grin. Belinda helps pass out glasses of lemonade while Grandpa goes inside to get dog bowls for Woof and Ruthie.

"Woof!" says my dog.

"Phew!" says Raafe. "Now that we've solved the Mariposa mystery, can we find out what happened to my drone? *Please?*"

"Of course," I say. "We should finish our drinks and go through the facts again."

"Maybe we should just go play some more," says Mariposa, taking long sips of water. "I feel better, and I bet the drone will turn up somewhere."

"A good detective never leaves a mystery unsolved," I say. "Just let me sit quietly for a minute and think about this troubling case." As I sip my lemonade and think about the clues, my pencil falls to the ground.

Everybody else is chattering and sipping water or lemonade.

I lean over to pick up the pencil, and Woof nudges me. "Okay, boy, you get it," I whisper in his ear. Still, I sneak a peek under the table. I chuckle because it reminds me of seeing everybody's shoes under the truck. Blue sneakers—Raafe; black lace-ups—Calvin; white with ponies—Anita B.; gray sneakers with white bunnies—Belinda Bundy. And one more . . .

Oh my! I think I know what happened!

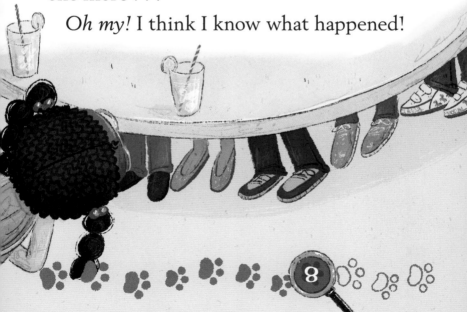

CHAPTER #9
THE SCENT OF THE CRIME

WHILE THE others are busy sipping their drinks, my mind whirs with facts and clues.

I whisper to Woof, "I think we're real close to solving this crime."

He nudges my notebook toward me. "Yes, Woof," I say in a soft voice, "let's review my notes from *The Big Book of Detective Tips*."

Notes from *The Big Book of Detective Tips*:

How to Map the Crime Scene

1. Ask yourself: How? Why? When? and Where? ✓

2. Now draw a picture of where everything and everyone was. ✓

3. Look for what's out of place or doesn't belong. ✓

4. Don't forget to use your eyes, ears, and even your nose. ✓

Here's how I followed
the tips:

1. Pictured the scene of the crime
2. Asked everyone questions
3. Drew a diagram of <u>where</u> the
   drone disappeared
4. Figured out <u>when</u> the drone
   must have gone missing and
   where everyone was when it
   happened

"But *why?*" I ask. "That question had me stumped."

"Me too!" says Raafe. Calvin and Belinda Bundy nod. Anita B. scowls, and her grumpy dog barks, "Gruff! Gruff! Gruff!"

I smile at them and say, "That's when the most important question hit me: What is out of place?"

Anita B. huffs. "I hope you're not trying to pin the theft on me again!" she says.

"No, Anita, I'm not," I say, then I look from face to face before continuing.

Woof thumps his tail. I rub his fur. "You're right, boy!" I say. "When I looked under the truck, I saw everyone's feet. Remember the shoes, boy?" I ask.

"Woof!" he barks.

"I remember that!" says Belinda Bundy. "I looked under the truck, too. What's so important about everyone's shoes?"

"Well," I begin, and take a look under the table, "I see all the same feet, plus a pair that wasn't there under the truck."

Belinda gets out of her seat and is hop-hop-hopping again when I sit up. This time without her pogo stick. She's always calm when there's a mystery to be solved because she knows Woof and I are great detectives. Raafe sits next to Calvin, looking sad. Anita B. turns to me. Of course, her arms are crossed.

"Hurry up and solve this mystery so I can go home!" she says with a scowl.

Woof sniffs the air and we share a look. Then he crawls under the table. "Mariposa, where did you go while the rest of us were at the truck?" I ask gently.

CHAPTER #10

RED HERRING OR RED-HANDED?

"I DIDN'T go anywhere," she says quickly. "I didn't!" Mariposa jumps up from the table.

"But when I looked under the truck, I saw everybody's shoes," I told her, "except for your sparkly ones. I don't believe you were there with the rest of us."

Mariposa swallows hard and her cheeks redden.

Anita B. narrows her eyes. "I knew it! She's

the crook, and she tried to blame me!"

Woof returns from beneath the table with Mariposa's bag. He barks, "Woof!"

"Do you mind?" I ask.

Mariposa shakes her head so I grab the bag, open it, and remove what's inside.

The remote-control drone!

Raafe springs from his seat and races to his drone. So does Ruthie. *Sniff-sniff-sniff!*

"Arf!" says Ruthie.

"Ruthie wasn't only barking because your

blood sugar was low. She could also still smell the old lamb scent on the drone from Raafe's book bag," I say. "Just like this morning with Zach. Ruthie helped solve the case!"

"The nose knows!" Calvin says with a grin.

Mariposa drops her head. When she looks up, she seems miserable. "I'm so sorry," she says to me. Then she turns to Raafe.

"I did it for a joke, at first. I wanted to see if Wednesday was a good enough detective to figure it out, like Shirley Hurley from my favorite mystery books. And Anita B. was the perfect red herring," she says.

"Are you calling me a fish?" says Anita B. "A herring is a fish, right?"

Gruff barks, "Gruff! Gruff!"

"In a mystery book, a red herring is the person everyone thinks did the crime," I say. "Only it's a distraction from who really did it. Did you really plan to keep Raafe's drone, Mariposa?"

"I didn't realize how sad Raafe would be," she says. "Honest! I really didn't! Then everything started happening too fast. When I made it look like poor Anita B. was guilty, I realized it was too much."

Mariposa looks down at Ruthie. "All I wanted after that was for everybody to leave the patio so I could return the drone," she says.

"Raafe, I'm really sorry. Really, really sorry," says Mariposa. "And you too, Wednesday and Anita B. Can you ever, ever forgive me?"

OH NO! ONLY ONE MORE CHAPTER LEFT. DO YOU THINK WEDNESDAY AND MARIPOSA WILL STAY FRIENDS?

CHAPTER #11

PEACE

AFTER A moment, Raafe sets his smelly drone on the table, puts his hands together the same way we do in prayer, and says, "Salaam. That means peace. I forgive you. I'm just glad to have it back!"

Mariposa sighs and says, "Thank you, Raafe."

"Anita! Anita!" a voice sings out from the end of the walk.

"Come along, Anita," calls her mom. "Time for our mermaid lessons."

"Momma!" says Anita B. She turns to me and says, "Told you I have something very important to do."

"MERMAID LESSONS!" we all say at the same time.

"We might be going on a vacation to the ocean, and when we do, I want to swim like a mermaid," huffs Anita B. before spinning around and running toward her mother. Gruff barks once and chases after her.

"Thanks, sis, for figuring that out," Raafe says. "Now, I'm starved. Grandpa, can we have more snacks?"

Grandpa laughs and goes inside. Raafe and Calvin go back into the yard to play with the drones. Belinda Bundy gets back on her pogo stick.

"I knew you'd solve the case," she tells me. "You're way better than any detective in a book! I need to get home, but I'll come back later." Belinda Bundy waves as she *boing-boing-boings* across the walk.

Mariposa sits back down at the patio table.

She looks sad.

Ruthie nuzzles up beside her, quiet for the first time since they arrived. I sit down in the chair beside Mariposa, and Woof puts his head in my lap.

"Don't be sad," I say, reaching out to touch Mariposa's hand. "Everything's fine."

She looks up, and soon we're both smiling.

"Sorry," she says.

I squeeze her hand. Then I grin and ask, "So, *am* I?"

"Are you what?" Mariposa asks.

"Am I as good as that Shirley Hurley girl from your book?" I say.

She takes a moment, takes a deep breath, and blows it out. "I  learned today that the Wednesday and Woof Detective Agency is for real," she says. "And you're *way* better than Shirley Hurley!"

I look at Woof. He looks at me.

What more can I say?

We can't help it. The number one detective agency in the whole wide world—well, at least our neighborhood—is Wednesday and Woof!

CONGRATULATIONS!

You've read **11** chapters,

87 pages,

and **4,013** words!

What a *PUP-TASTIC* effort!

If you've read books one and two, you've read 11,119 words!

What mysteries will you solve next?

Arf! Arf! Arf!

Woof! *Woof!*

FUN AND GAMES FOR DETECTIVES IN TRAINING

THINK

Detectives like Wednesday and Woof are always curious. They ask lots of questions when they are learning about a case. Think of something you'd like to know more about. Then make a list of five questions you'd ask to kick-start your investigation!

FEEL

Have you ever been the new person in a group like Mariposa? Write about one thing someone did to help you feel better about being new.

ACT

In this book, Wednesday uses drawings to help her find the missing drone. Here's a way you can practice your observation skills: Make a map of your kitchen. Note all the important details. Then leave the room and ask someone to move three things around. Can you spot what's out of place?

My name is **SHERRI WINSTON**. I grew up in Muskegon Heights, Michigan, where there are lots of lakes and parks and beaches. My favorite color is pink and my favorite books are filled with mystery and adventure. I can't wait to share more stories with you guys, my new friends.

My name is **GLADYS JOSE**. I grew up in Orlando, Florida, where each summer my friends and I had adventures pretending we were secret agents. Now I create art every day, with the help of my four-year-old daughter, who has taken on the role of art director, a.k.a. she tells me when I need to redraw something.